About the Author

He's a young storyteller. His life and work is always drawn from passion. He is aspiring to be a director in the film industry. But also a storyteller. His passion is always creating original stories which he draws from his love of superheroes and also his life experiences that he has gone through.

Divided

Bradley J Ellis

Divided

Olympia Publishers
London

www.olympiapublishers.com
OLYMPIA PAPERBACK EDITION

A CIP catalogue record for this title is
available from the British Library.

ISBN: 978-1-80439-343-7

This is a work of fiction.
Names, characters, places and incidents originate from the writer's
imagination. Any resemblance to actual persons, living or dead, is
purely coincidental.

First Published in 2023

Olympia Publishers
Tallis House
2 Tallis Street
London
EC4Y 0AB

Printed in Great Britain

Dedication

This book is dedicated to my mother, Louise Ellis. My real-life superhero.

Chapter 1

It's a Monday morning in a little town called Paignton; a cold breeze floats through the streets like a breath been taken. It's the middle of winter, with people wrapped up warm in coats and scarves, rushing into their buildings for warmth.

Then a guy wearing blue jeans, a black jean jacket and brown shoes is walking towards a college building named South Devon College with his grey headphones on, listening to music. He attends there three times a week, studying Film Production.

As soon as the guy took his first step into the building, he took big breath in and exhales.

"That was brisk," said the guy.

The guy walks further in, past an elevator, with every step hitting the floor loudly, creating an echo within his environment; the echo is caused by the smart wingtip shoes he wears. He approaches the stairs at the end of the room, and a man who has brown hair with a small beard, wearing a leather jacket approaches the guy calling out his name.

"Drake. Drake."

Drake begins to walk up the stairs with his headphones still on, oblivious to what is happening around him. Suddenly Drake feels a soft pressure on his shoulder, revealing the man with his hand on Drake's shoulder. Drake turns around, not too pleased to see the person who is in front of him. He takes off his headphones.

"How can I help you. Tony?" Drake asked.

Tony Marigold his tutor/lecture – Drake isn't too pleased to see him.

Tony asks, "How are you feeling today? I know it's not been easy but—"

Before Tony could finish his sentence Drake comes back stern with, "I'm fine."

"Look no-one will judge if you need more time," Tony replies trying to reassure him, console him, all in one.

But Drake comes back with, "I have had my time, now I need to get back to work." Drake pushes Tony's hand off his shoulder and continues to walk back up the stairs, At the bottom of the stairs is Tony, with a worried expression on his face. Drake turns around, puts his headphones back on and walks away.

Drake walks through a crowded hallway full of people, His hands and forehead start to sweat like he's about to fill a pool full of water. He starts to look around very anxiously, Drake can't handle social groups as it is, let alone with what's recently just happened to him. Drake freezes in his position trying to process everything, and without him realising, a young lady with blonde hair and a slim build, wearing a blue shirt with a flower in the middle of it and a black jacket, with a handbag by her side, appears in front of him with a curious look of concern on her face.

"Drake."

He doesn't respond he's oblivious to everything like he's in a trance, then the young lady raises her hand and clicks her finger three times to and calls out "Drake," in a louder tone.

Drake awakens and notices her. Ronnie. Ronnie Edwards, Drake's closest friend of a year. Drake didn't know anyone when he moved down to Paignton from Berkshire about four years ago, and Ronnie was the first person he met when he started college. Drake takes off his headphones, "When did you get there?" he says, confused on how she got in front of him so easily.

She replies, just as confused, saying, "I just walked up to you calling your name you weren't responding to me."

He turned to her and said, "I'm sorry, I wasn't all with it, I have a lot on my mind."

She starts to come to the realisation of what's going on. "I understand, Drake, after losing your mother it hurts like hell for a while, you don't understand why her, and you feel like it's not real. It's also like you haven't adjusted to this new life."

Drake's eyes look away from her, trying to be respectful but also trying to block out what she's saying. Suddenly his phone starts to vibrate; the number belongs to a person called Andrew Loid. Drake's face went from sadness to anger in under a few seconds. He pressed the decline button and starts to put his headphones back on and says, "Look I know you mean well, but I just don't need this right now, I'm sorry," and walks away.

Chapter 2

Drake is sitting at the very back of the room in the corner, like a shadow against the wall. He feels lost and confused due to the death of his mother. He keeps seeing flashes of her in his mind, painful memories which he tries to bury. Drake just sits there, daydreaming with headphones on, trying to block out his surroundings. Ronnie goes to the back of the room walking slowly towards him, but then stops and she comes to the realisation that nothing she says will help him. She starts to frown and turns around to go back to her seat, but before she could reach her seat Tony intercepts her like a police officer would stop someone on the street. She looks how Drake feels – sad.

Tony says to her, "Has he said anything to you?"

She sighs and replies, "Only that he doesn't want to hear what we have to say right now, but I know he feels lost and he doesn't have any hope or anything, for that matter, to keep him preoccupied."

Tony's face changes from concerned to thoughtful. "I might have an idea that might set him on a better path. I just need to sort out the details, let me try something," Tony replied with a surprising idea that sprung in his mind.

The following week on Monday morning, Drake walks into class like it's an average day. Tony, at the front of the class, asks Drake to wait outside. Drake turns around and heads back through the door sighing, thinking he is going to get another concerned chat. Tony walks out and asks Drake to follow him. Whilst walking with Tony, Drake strongly says, "If this is another chat about my wellbeing, I don't want to hear it."

Tony quickly replies saying, "Nope it's not that. I have an opportunity that I want you take. It will help complete the rest of this year's course in one project and it will help with what you are going through."

Drake has a confused face on him and realises he has been led into a meeting room. The room has a large digital screen at the end of the room with a web cam connected to it. Also, there is a large table in the middle with multiple chairs around it.

"What am I doing in here Tony?" Drake asks sternly,

"It's a meeting room and you're in for a meeting."

Drake has a confused look on his face. "Who am I having a meeting with?"

Tony looks at him and smiles, like he is pleased with what he has done. "I have got you a meeting with a record label who is looking for a student who can produce and direct their artists single and I have chosen you".

Drake looks at Tony and dramatically says to him, "Hang on, I never agreed to this."

Tony quickly replying with, "No, but you need to make up some work experience and you need to complete the units, so this how it's going to be."

Drake sharply says "But—" and Tony interrupts him like he's got no choice in the matter.

"No ifs and no BUTS, you are doing this, so get ready, get your business face on and do the job." Tony leaves the room and Drake turns the screen on.

Drake starts to get nervous; his heart starts to beat faster like a drum at a rock concert. Then a call request comes in, Drake breathes in heavily and exhales loudly, takes five seconds to compose himself and then presses 'Answer'.

A man in black suit, with brown hair and a purple tie pops up on the screen. Drake feels like he is in his first formal meeting of his life. His heart is still beating quite fast but before Drake says anything, the man introduces himself.

"Good morning, I'm guessing. Different time zones. Very confusing," he says in an American accent, to break the ice. Drake looks at the big screen and replies, "Good evening or maybe early morning would be the correct term. My name is Drake Reynolds and you are Mr..."

"My name is Roman Walters. I'm the record producer for Walters Records. I'm guessing you have been told why we are meeting today," he says passionately.

Drake says directly, "Yes, it was a last-minute decision. So how can I help?" Drake is only asking to be polite – he knows why he's here.

Roman puts his hands together, creating a ball shape with his hands like he's an evil villain and replies, "I'm going to cut right to it. I have an artist who has a new single out and we want a music video created, but we want to also give young creative minds a chance to produce and direct one for us."

Drake puts his arm on the desk and has his leg on top of his leg trying to gain some control in this meeting.

"Well, if I was to direct this music video, I would expect full creative control, also I would have to meet this artist before we shoot, to get her opinion on this as well, because I will not work under restrictions and I want to know I have control of this project," Drake says in a demanding way. Roman breathes in and out, like he feels he has lost control of the negotiation, but realises that this is the best he is going to get.

"Okay, you have yourself a deal. Damn, you really know how to get what you want don't you?"

Drake puts his foot down and leans on his knees, having remembered who his mentor was and replies cryptically, "I was taught to always remain in control of any situation. So, who is the artist I would be working with?"

Roman leans back in his seat and picks up a piece of paper with an image of a young white lady, slim build, black hair and blue eyes.

"You will be working with Grace Fletcher," he announces to him, in a direct way. As soon as Drake heard the name, he instantly knew who she was. He has listened to her music a lot throughout his life and she is also the same age as Drake – twenty years old. Drake's eyes widened in shock, his heart speeds up again and his hands become sweaty. He starts to speak, but finds it hard to say anything.

"I umm would need to meet her as soon as possible." Roman gives a sudden smile, knowing that Drake is shocked and surprised by the way he reacted to the announcement, and then replies, saying, "She will be in the UK in a few days. She will come to the college to sit with you and hear your idea."

Drake's heart is still sped up because he used to have a crush on her for a few months; he can't believe that it is happening, he feels like it's a dream that he hasn't woken up from yet. Drake is frozen in an instant, with Roman asking, "Mr Reynolds are you all right?"

Drake shakes his head like he is bringing himself back to reality and says, "Oh yes, sorry, I will be ready by then thank you."

Roman replies with the intention of encouragement, "Good luck, Mr Reynolds."

The video call ends, leaving Drake stunned still. As soon as the screen went black, he breathed in heavily and out strongly. He is now left to plan this new project, realising he doesn't know where to start.

Chapter 3

It's a Friday morning, it has been three days since Drake had his meeting with Roman Walters' record label. Drake wakes up, stretching his arms like he was reaching for something. Drake isn't happy. because he hasn't had much sleep since his mother died. He reaches for his phone which is placed on his bed side table, his phone lit up and there were two messages left on there from Andrew Loid which says to him:

Andrew Loid:

Listen Drake I know I am not your
favourite person but I am here if you
Want to talk.

Andrew Loid:

Drake there is something we need to
discuss please contact me

Drake instantly ignores the messages that Andrew left him and gets up to get dressed.

He heads downstairs to the kitchen and notices his nan sitting down at the table, having a cup of coffee. She looks like all the energy has been drained from her. Drake goes to the fridge to get some orange juice. He keeps it in the side of the door where he keeps the milk and orange squash. He pulls it out and his nan asks him, "How are you feeling today, Drake?"

Drake has a serious facial expression, which he tends to

have every day and he replies, "I am fine, just a bit tired, that's all. Got my meeting with Grace Fletcher in about half an hour, so I got to get moving". He walks towards to door leaving the kitchen, but his nan says to him, "Listen, I know you're going through a tough time right now, I get it but you don't have to go through this alone. I'm here whenever you need me."

Drake doesn't even face his nan fully just turns his head slightly to left like he is eavesdropping on a conversation and just replies with, "I know – I got to go, I won't be late home." He heads to the door to put on his jean jacket and brown wingtip shoes and when he gets up, he looks in the mirror in front of him. He looks at himself and starts to evaluate his life and who he has become. He stands there for a solid few seconds, smartens up his jacket tightly and leaves to go to college.

Drake walks towards the meeting room in his college. He looks into the room, noticing a woman, who has a slim build with black hair, wearing a leather jacket and jeans, sitting in the chair, waiting for him. He starts to panic but takes a deep breath in and deep breath out and walks into the room, confident, like he has a split personality, but Drake is used to having to create a façade, due to what he used to do back in Berkshire.

"Hello, Miss Fletcher. My name's Drake Reynolds, please, call me Drake," he says, whilst walking to his seat. Drake starts to set up his laptop, whilst Grace replies directly, "Okay Drake, and please call me Grace as well."

Drake nods his head and directs Grace towards the digital screen with his PowerPoint on.

"So Grace, I've heard the song and here's my idea. What I was thinking is that the video could be about social status, and that we show each element of the social hierarchy; we have you as a character that goes through the struggles of that, whilst also having shots of you singing and it passes back and forth."

Grace looks intrigued by the idea and has a passionate expression on her face whilst saying, "I like the idea. It's very current in society today, and I think it will work with what the song represents. I am onboard with this idea, so what are the next steps?"

Drake feels a lot more relaxed knowing that Grace liked his idea and feels appreciated. Drake responds saying, "So what I will need to do is some research into the idea and then do some location scouting, which I'll probably do next week, so I'll keep you up to date on the process."

Grace looks at Drake now with a confused expression. "I think you misunderstood what I meant when I asked 'what are the next steps', because I was hoping to get more involved, like maybe come with you on location scouting, if that's all right?"

Drake looks at her for a few seconds trying to determine if it would be appropriate or necessary for her to come along, but he comes to conclusion that maybe he needs to adapt to change and says, "I normally work alone, it's how my process works, but maybe I can do with some help."

Grace's facial expression changes to a smile and then she replies, "Okay then, what day are we going?"

Drake starts to think of a good day to do it and comes out and says, "I think Monday will be a good time to go because then I will have time to do pre-production and research afterwards."

Grace looks at Drake nods her head and says, "Okay then, I'll see you on Monday thank you for letting me be more involved." Grace puts out her hand and Drake gives a firm handshake and says, "No worries, I'll see you Monday."

She then grabs her stuff and walks out of the room with Drake still in the room, clearing everything up, and it takes a minute to get more relaxed, because he felt quite tense during the meeting.

The next day hits like the speed of light and Drake is stressed about the project. He starts pacing around his room, trying to approach how his day is meant to go. Drake has dealt with worse things in his life, but the one thing he hasn't dealt with is his grief for his mother and now a girl has been brought into his life. Suddenly a knock-on Drake's bedroom hits out of the blue, Drake walks to his door and opens it, and his nan is in the doorway.

"Are you all right, Drake? I can hear the ceiling creaking a lot," says his nan. The house is quite new, but some of the floorboards in his house are quite loose which creates the creaking sound in the floor.

Drake replies honestly, "Just nerves, I guess. I'm not used working with someone again, I work better alone." His nan gives him a sympathetic look and gives him some advice.

"Look, life is hard and life is changing, you need to be able to keep moving forward and accept that change is inevitable and living is a choice. You just need to decide whether you want to live or keep being stuck in an endless traumatic moment."

Drake looks at his nan feeling inspired, but still feeling lost in the process; suddenly, Drake's phone vibrates. He takes his phone out of his pocket and looks at it.

Unknown Number:
I'm at the college where are you?

Drake grabs his backpack and jacket and says to his nan, "Thanks for the advice but I have to go."

He walks past his nan down the stairs and gets his wing tip shoes on, like he is in a rush to leave. He grabs the handle of the door and leaves to go to meet Grace.

Chapter 4

Drake arrives in front of South Devon College with headphones on. He notices Grace standing in front of a Black BMW. He takes his headphones off and Grace quickly says, "You ready to go?"

Drake looks at her with a judgemental look on his face and replies, "Yes I am, but we're not going in the car."

Grace has a confused look on her face as to why Drake wouldn't get in the car and asks him, "Why? What's wrong with the car?"

Drake quickly responds to her comment, trying not to sound too judgemental. "Nothing – I have just been in enough fancy cars to last me a lifetime, and I don't want special treatment because I am working with you."

Grace looks at Drake with a death stare and sharply responds, "So your pride is what's keeping you from getting in this car. Okay, so what do you suggest we do then?"

Drake gets a smug look on his face, whilst saying, "We're getting the train."

Grace looks at Drake with disappointment; she doesn't really like getting on public transportation. She replies, annoyed, "Fine," then they leave to get on the number 22 bus to the train station.

The bus pulls into the Paignton bus station, the 22 is full of passengers. Drake sat with his headphones on the entire ride and didn't communicate with Grace at all. She gets up to leave but is squished back down into her seat. The bus is like the tube in London, in the early mornings, cramped and rushed. She is easily getting frustrated trying to leave and looks at Drake like she doesn't have the patience for this. He instructs her, "Move now," and shoves Grace in the empty gap between people and then follows soon after. They managed to get off the bus and Grace gives daggers at Drake and says, "Wouldn't it have been easier to have taken the car here at least?"

Drake reminds her, "Like I said, I have been in enough of them, I don't want to do that anymore."

She looks at him again but doesn't respond and starts to follow him towards the train station. Drake walks towards a machine and takes out his wallet to get cash for a ticket to get to Plymouth. It costs him £12 for a ticket there and back. Drake says to her, "You're up – remember to get a return ticket, it's easier that way."

She still has the frustrated attitude that is creating tension between Drake and Grace. She grabs her ticket and follows Drake into the station.

There are a few people on the other side of the track standing, whilst two people are leaning against the wall, drinking and eating. They both sit down on the bench and tension is high between the both of them.

Grace moves closer towards Drake, like they're almost joined at the hip, and says in a sarcastic way, "You know we would probably already be there right now, you know, that right?" and Drake with no care in what she's saying faces forward with his leg on top of the other and replies, "Yeah I know," and then silence falls upon them both.

The train pulls into Paignton train station and they both get up and grab their bags, and Drake instructs her to follow him. She follows, but she doesn't appreciate what's happening.

They both walk towards the door and push the button to open the door, which made a loud noise like a loud breath has been exhaled. They both get on the train and sit opposite each other.

Grace leans in on the table separating them and says, "How long is this going to take?" and Drake looks back smugly, knowing she won't like the answer and says, "Just over an hour."

Grace has a shocked look on her face and replies sternly, saying, "What the fuck, we could have been here and headed back just from the length of this train journey alone. But all because of your pride, we have wasted time. What am I meant to do for the next hour?"

Drake looks at her and makes a suggestion. "I don't know maybe sleep, listen to music that's usually what I do." Grace leans back in her chair and faces the window, then the train begins to depart from the station.

Drake and Grace arrive in Plymouth, Grace is agitated from the long journey and Drake is still lacking in communication with Grace. When they both leave the train station, they start walking towards the shopping complex. They start to go down the high street where it's quite busy, and full of people doing their shopping, along the way they see loads of shops like Top Shop and Game. Whilst they're walking, Grace notices two people, one woman and one male, wearing old and ragged clothes, wrapped in a sleeping bag, one of them being a child. Whilst Drake continues to walk on Grace walks towards the two people, she feels sorry for them. She crouched down and grabs all her loose change from her purse; she noticed a cup on the floor and put the change in there. As soon as the money hit the bottom of the cup the woman started to cry and said, "Thank you," three times. Grace looks at the woman saying, "It's my pleasure."

Drake realises that Grace isn't following him anymore when he realises she's stopped complaining. He turns around and sees her crouching in front of a woman and child. He thought, 'Well that was unexpected.'

Grace moves towards the child and pulls out a key ring. The key ring has a sun with a circle around it. Grace then says, "This is something that helps me through the tough times. The sun represents the light of the universe and the circle is meant to represent the darkness and as you can see it shines brighter then darkness. My mum gave it to me when I was your age and I'm going to give it to you."

She hands the key ring to the boy and the boy responds saying, "Thank you, miss." Grace says, "You're very welcome," and gets back up and starts to head towards Drake.

Drake looks at her surprised with what she did and says "So you do have a heart." Grace looks at him with a smile and then begin to carry on walking.

Drake and Grace are halfway done through their location scouting and Grace is beginning to feel tired. She implores drake and says, "Please can we take a break, I'm hungry and I am tired, please." Drake looks at her and agrees, saying, "Okay then, there is a restaurant round the corner called Nando's, we can get some food there."

They both head towards Nando's and Grace feels relieved to finally be getting some rest; they both head inside and wait for a table. The restaurant is very busy and very loud it's like you can barely hear yourself think.

A waitress comes up and says, "Table for two?" and Drake replies with "Yes, thank you." They both walk towards a table numbered 27 and as they both sit down the waitress says to them, "When you're ready to order go up to the counter."

Drake replies with, "Thank you." The waitress walks away, and Grace looks at Drake, then leans in, saying "It's very busy in here, I'm guessing this place is popular." Drake, with a small grin, says, "Something like that," and puts up his menu to his face.

After six minutes of looking through the menu, Drake asks, "Have you decided what you want yet?" Grace replies saying, "I'm having some peri-peri chips with five chicken wings and a refillable drink." Drake then gets up to go order. Whilst he is in the queue Grace stares at Drake like she's scanning him trying to understand him. Within no time he returns back to his seat with Grace still staring at him.

"What? Why are you staring at me" he asks, confused, and she replies, "What's your deal?"

Drake, still confused, asks "My deal?" and she looks at him and replies, "You seem nice at some moments, but it seems like you hate me for some reason. Why is that?"

Drake looks at her trying to find the words but then he says, "I don't hate you, how can I? I don't even know you."

Grace looks confused and pressures onwards. "Then what is it?"

Drake, not knowing what to say, starts to think back to his mother knowing that's where the conversation is leading. He breathes in heavily, and then takes a huge breath out and opens up.

"Okay. About 2 months ago, I lost my mother to cancer."

Grace quickly responds with, "I'm so sorry."

Drake starts to get emotional; his facial expression saddens, and his posture loosens and he says, "No, it's all right. You know, I used to be really kind and sweet, and an overall nice guy. My mother helped guide me throughout my life and made me a better person. But when she died, I lost my way."

Grace responds trying to let him know she understands "I know what it's like to lose a parent – I lost my father a few years ago. Car accident. He had his headphones on and was walking across the street, and a car came towards him, and her brakes failed, and my father was killed instantly."

Drake sympathises with her "I'm sorry to hear that."

Grace continues to speak. "Thank you, but the point I'm trying to make is I understand and I was changed for a while myself, but I made my way back to who I am and I think you will, too."

Drake starts to feel more comfortable around her and asks her something. "Does the pain ever go away?"

Grace responds with honest words. "The pain of losing a parent never goes away. It will always be with you but it will be manageable, it will get easier. But you will have your good days and your bad ones. But the pain doesn't go away completely. No" Drake starts to feel disappointed, but also a lot more calm and relaxed, knowing someone else understands him.

The food arrives at the table with Graces five chicken wings, peri-peri chips and her refillable drink and Drake's refillable drink and mash potato and sweet potato fries. They both start to look happy when the food arrives and over the course of the meal they start to bond, to feel more comfortable around one another.

Towards the end of the meal, after having a few laughs and bonding with one another, Grace asks, "What made you want to open up to me?"

Drake looks at her dead in the eyes with a smile on his face and responds, "When you helped those two homeless people you showed your true colours, and for some reason I felt that I could tell you something personal that I haven't spoken to anyone about before. I don't know, I think it just felt right"

Grace smiles at Drake and says, "Thank you." Drake then asks Grace a question, "So why did you open up to me then? You didn't have to, and I came across a bit mean, so why?"

Grace looks at Drake in the eyes and says, "Because you told me the hardest thing in your life right now and as soon as you said that I knew you weren't a bad person."

Drake feels a sense of warmth and comfort knowing that Grace saw the true Drake for the first time and replies saying, "Thank you, you don't understand how much that means to me."

Drake gets up out of his chair ready to leave when Grace asks, "Where you going?"

Drake replies, saying, "We are leaving to head back."

Grace looked confused, thinking they haven't paid the

bill, so she states, "But we haven't paid the bill though."

Drake replies, saying, "You pay when you order, I paid don't worry about it." Grace looks at him, her cheeks are turning red like she feels something towards him, and replies to him saying, "Thank you."

They both head out to get the train back to Paignton and they walk up the hill with the sun setting, and for the first time since they met, they are finally getting along.

Chapter 5

It's been over two weeks since Drake and Grace went location scouting and a lot has happened in this time. Drake started and finished production on the music video for Grace's record label, and he is in the stages of editing it together. Throughout the time Drake and Grace have managed to get closer more then they realise. They have been out bowling with one another, they managed to go drinking down the pub and also went to the cinema at one point.

Its Sunday morning and Drake wakes up; since he met Grace, he's been getting good sleep. He goes downstairs to get a drink of orange juice and puts some toast on. Whilst he waits, he texts Grace, letting her know that he is almost finished editing and is asking her to celebrate the end of music video project that they have done together.

Drake Reynolds:

Hey I'm almost done editing, you want to celebrate?

As Drake waits for a response from Grace, his toast makes a ding sound and the toast shoots up from the toaster. Whilst they are in mid-air Drake catches them and puts them on the plate. His phone starts to vibrate again. It's a response saying:

Grace Fletcher:

Yes, I would love to do so how about we go to the beach have a couple of drinks and watch the sun go down

Drake's smile widens when he sees the message, he feels a warmth, and finally that his life is on track again. Drake then replies:

Drake Reynolds:

Sounds fun see you there!

Drake finally finishes his work on the music video; he takes a massive breath in and out, to finally relieve all the stress. Drake closes his laptop and heads to the bathroom to have a shower. He takes off his shirt, and we see that Drake has multiple scars on his back, chest, arms and shoulders. Throughout his childhood, he was always put in intense situations and sometimes he got injured. Drake takes the rest of his clothes off and has a shower.

Drake exits the shower and goes to the bedroom to get dressed. Without knowing it, Drake puts on some smart clothes like he is dressed to impress. He puts on a red, chequered shirt with rolled-up sleeves, black jeans and his wingtip shoes. He looks at himself in the mirror, and puts some hair product in and sprays himself with cologne. He looks back in the mirror and his heart is racing, but tries to remain calm.

It's almost sunset as Drake arrives at Goodrington beach and he see Grace walking towards him. As soon as they see each other they give each other a big hug, lasting a bit longer than a normal hug would.

When they get back to eye contact, they both give a nervous smile and Drake says, "Why don't we head over to there?" pointing to a clear space where no rocks lie. He grabbed the beach cooler from Grace which she had brought with her – He has to be a gentleman and help her. They both head over to the spot that they both agreed upon. Drake lays down two beach towels and they both sit in front of the sunset. Drake opens the cooler and pulls a champagne bottle he states, "We really are celebrating, aren't we?"

Grace starts laughing but in a flirty way, replying, "I guess we are."

Drake pulls out the two glasses that were in the cooler and says, "I've got a trick I want to show you."

Grace is confused as to what's happening. Drake asks "Did you bring the knife, as I asked you too?"

Grace looks at him; she was very sceptical about bringing it. But she replies, saying, "Yes, it's in the cooler."

Drake stands up and picks up the knife and very confidently grabs the champagne bottle; he places the knife below the cork. With a powerful slice below the cork, the cork is released and shot into mid-air like a gun shot, with the champagne fizzing over.

Grace was very impressed with how he did that and asks, "How did you learn how to do that?" Drake looked at her, smiled, and said, "Something I picked up along the way."

Drake leans down pours a glass for Grace and then sits back down and pours a glass for himself. They touch glasses together and both say, "Cheers" and they both drink.

Drake sits there, thinking to himself what to say because he is well nervous, so he asks her. "So what are you going to do now, when you head back to America?"

Grace looks at him with an agenda at hand and she replies, "I don't know – I was actually thinking maybe I could stay in the UK for a bit longer."

Drake is confused at why she would want to stay here, and then he replies, "Why would you want to stay here for longer? Your life is in America."

Grace looks at him and she brushes her black hair behind her ear, and her cheeks begins to turn red, and says "Because I want to be with you.

Drake looks at her as he is confused with what she said, and he replies to her saying, "Well, we can talk all the time. Friends move away, but still remain in contact."

Grace looks at him; she feels like he misunderstood what she was saying, so she replies with, "No, Drake. I want to be more than friends. Do you get what I mean?"

Grace looks into Drake's eyes and Drake replies, "I get it you want to be best friends, which is cool with me."

Grace feels like he is really misunderstanding what's going on. She shakes her head and says, "No." Then she leans in to Drake and gives him a kiss on the lips. Drake feels a sudden warmth, whilst kissing Grace, her wet red lips on his and making him feel something he hasn't felt before. The passionate kiss lasts about thirty seconds before she leans back. Drake was surprised with what just happened and is left speechless.

Grace looks at Drake and asks him, "Do you understand now?" Drake's face is still in shock and nods his head and says, "Umm, umm, I, umm need to go, sorry."

Drake quickly jumps to his feet and walks off, back home. Grace feels humiliated and left distraught. She calls for a car to pick her up and she heads back to her hotel.

It's the morning after Drake is left surprised by what Grace confessed to him. He is still in shock after what happened but today is also an important day. Drake has to showcase his final product to his class. Drake then goes through his morning routine and then gets ready to leave to go to college.

When Drake arrives at college, he heads up to the cinema room where his class is. He has got everything prepared, but his mind is somewhere else; his heart is pounding, he doesn't know if its nerves for the showcase or something else. He arrives at the cinema room right on time and his teacher, Tony Marigold, is waiting for him.

He looks at Drake and says, "Are you ready to showcase your work?"

Drake looks at him and says, "Yes, I'm ready." Drake is sweating and still freaking out, but he has to pull himself together to get through this. Tony looks at Drake and says, "Let's get going then."

Drake and Tony walk into the screening room – it looks exactly like a cinema, with a big screen at the front and loads of seats facing it. Tony heads to seating area where the class is, and Drake heads to the front and plugs in his MacBook and loads up his presentation.

Drake addresses the audience by saying, "Good morning everyone, and welcome to my showcase. Today I will be showing you the music video I have created and want to hear your feedback, so please enjoy and thank you." Drake sits back in his seat plays the music video.

Once the music video was ended, he stood back up and everyone in the room started clapping, but before Drake can say anything his teacher, Tony, said, "Drake before we move forward, there is something, I would like to show you."

Drake looks confused and asks, "What is it?"

Tony has a worried expression on his face but comes out and says, "There is something I need to show you. I was only ever allowed to show you this when there comes a time you need guidance the most. I realise now that after this project is done, you're going to feel like crap, so take a seat."

Drake sits down and is massively confused with what's going on and says, "What are you on about?" and suddenly a video pops up with Drake's mother's face on it.

His heart started pounding faster than ever, his hands began to sweat and he asks "What is this?" and Tony was worried but he said "Just watch."

The video began playing and his mother started to speak to him.

She said, "My beautiful boy, I understand you must be lost, and I know what you have had to witness is enough to drive anyone down a line of depression. But you have been a beacon of light in my darkness and you have helped me in so many ways that I am proud of you. I want you to know that wherever I go, I will always love you and I'll always be looking down on you because I'm never too far away. You were my rock and now you have to keep on living even though I'm not here, because life is more than me. Life is about change, something you don't like but you need to embrace it, and I know you are going to want to push people away but don't – lean on them for strength and guidance. When you find a girlfriend, you will learn to confide in her and she would be one lucky woman to have you as a partner, but remember never give up and that I'll always love you. You are a good person and you know what's right and what's wrong. You are a light bringer. I love you and, goodbye, my beautiful boy."

Drake starts crying in his seat and his friend Ronnie comes to his side.

She says, "Are you all right, Drake?"

Drake says, "That was the best gift anyone could ever give me."

Tony walks down to him. He looks worried that he might upset Drake, and he says, "I'm sorry."

Drake looks at Tony and says, "Thank you." He realises that he made a mistake and needs to rectify it. He looks at Tony and says, "There is something I need to do."

Drake runs past his teacher like lightning and rushes for the door; he bashes his way through it and runs out of the college, to get on a bus to Paignton. Drake is trying to ring Grace, but she isn't answering, and he starts to panic that she might have left. His leg is tapping out of nerves and his heart is back to pounding again. Drake see the number 22 bus. He pulls out his wallet and pays for his ticket. He rushes to his seat. His heart is pounding and he is starting to panic. The bus sets off on its journey.

Drake gets off at Paignton bus station and starts to run to the hotel Grace is staying at. He arrives at the hotel and rushes into the hotel like a headless chicken and presses the bell in lobby to get the receptionist's attention.

The receptionist comes out and says, "Can you please not ring the bell like that because–" and before he could finish Drake interrupts him and says, "Grace Fletcher is she still here?"

The receptionist says "She literally just left like two minutes ago."

He rushes back outside and looks around, he doesn't see her in sight, his facial expressions turn to sadness but then he sees the car that Grace's driver drives, and he stops in front of it like he has the power to do anything. He shouts "Grace," and then the side door opens, and Grace comes out of the car, confused at why he's here.

Grace looks at him and she says, "What are you doing here, Drake?"

Drake looks at her and starts to open his heart to her. "Listen, okay, I made a mistake, I should've never left that night, I'm sorry."

Grace still looks confused and asks him, "Why did you leave me there, then?"

Drake knew he had to be honest and he says, "Because I thought I would have ruined your life with all my baggage. I thought I was bad for you but then someone told me I need to confide in people and now I know I won't ruin your life, because if I was going to do that you would've stopped talking to me ages ago. I have felt nothing but pain before I met you and when you came into my life you gave me hope again and you gave me happiness and I can't give it up; I can't give you up because I like you more than a friend."

Grace looks at him and she feels overwhelmed with emotions and starts to shed a tear and says, "You do?"

Drake looks at Grace and grabs her by the hand and he replies, "Absolutely. So what do you say?"

Grace takes a second to think about it and she doesn't reply but she grabs Drake and passionately kisses Drake on the lips. They lock lips for thirty seconds and they look back into each other's eyes, and then they smile, realising the passion they have for one another.

Chapter 6

It has been one week since Drake and Grace got together, Drake is continuing to go to college and Grace has bought an apartment in Paignton and is staying in the UK for a while, continuing to create music in the local recording centre for the UK branch of Walters Records.

Drake has just finished college for the day and starts to head home. It's a breezy day and everyone is wrapped up warm in coats and scarves, due to it being winter. Most people are getting the 22-bus back home whilst others are getting lifts from their parents, which is causing traffic on the road. Drake walks home with his headphones on listening to his girlfriend's music. It normally takes ten minutes for Drake to get home, because he only lives around the corner.

Drake arrives home but notices a silver car in front of his house, which doesn't belong to anyone he lives with. In situations like this Drake was always taught to be suspicious and to be cautious. He walks slowly to the door like everything is in slow motion; he opens the door and hears people talking in the kitchen. He recognises the tone of the male voice in the kitchen. He takes off his backpack and heads in the kitchen, still being cautious about what's going on. He opens the door to the kitchen and sees a man with black hair, blue eyes, and wearing a black jumper and jogging bottoms. As soon as Drake sees him, he knew who he was, like an echo of his past coming back for him.

Drake says, in shock, "Dad."

His father, Rick Reynolds, turns around and says, "Hey son, I need your help."

Drake looks at his father in frustration and says to him, "How the hell can I help you, and if I could help, why should I help you?"

Rick has a worried look on his face and then draws his attention to Drake's nan, and says, "Jane, can I have a few minutes with him please its important?"

Jane looks at Drake with a concerned look on her face, knowing too well what Rick is like. Drake looks at his nan and reassures her, "I'll be fine. Give me a couple of minutes."

Jane leaves the room and closes the door behind her, leaving a room full of tension behind.

Drake looks at his father and starts to talk directly because he is no mood for small talk.

"What do you want?"

Rick takes a breath in and then exhales, like he is in a massive panic.

He says, "Your brother, Richard Small, he's in trouble and I'm not talking petty stuff. I mean he is in serious trouble and I need your help."

Drake looks at his father whilst feeling a sense of déjà vu and responds with sarcasm, "What, did he steal from a shop or maybe he got done beating another kid up?"

Rick rolls his eyes and starts to show more aggression in his tone, and puts his hands together like he is saying a prayer and he responds, "No goddamn it, he is working for a drug gang, to be more specific a local drug gang and his mum is worried, too. Please, Drake."

Drake starts to feel anxious; his hands start to shake, and his heart is pounding. Drake's past was defined by anger and hatred and he doesn't want to drag himself back into this life again.

Drake responds, "What can I do? I'm just a man who is in college, there's nothing I can do."

Rick looks at his son with respect and says, "Back when you were a boy you had a lot going on, but you always had time for people who were struggling themselves, and you helped set them on a better path. All I'm asking is you come with me, speak to him. Please."

Drake takes a moment to think before coming back with an answer. He says, "Fine, I'll come with you – but there are two things I want and if I don't get them, then you deal with him yourself."

Rick looks at his son with delight, knowing he will help, and says to him, "Sure, name it."

Drake looks at him dead in the eye to make sure he is genuine when Rick answers him. "I want full honesty from you all the way through – no lying. And I want to speak to his mother."

Rick rolls his eyes when he mentions speaking to his mother and Drake explains why, "Because she has the best knowledge on Richard, she knows him best. They are my terms, take it or leave it."

Rick takes a moment to think, and realises that he's the best hope in getting him back and replies, "Fine, we will set off in fifteen minutes, so get the things you need."

Drake turns around, and starts to feel discombobulated with

what's happening. He heads upstairs and immediately goes to the corner of his room and immediately goes to the corner of his room. He gently moves away his coffee table that's next to the side of his bed, and pulls back the carpet revealing the floorboards. Three of the floorboards are loose and concealing something underneath them. Drake grabs the screwdriver that he keeps on the bookcase for emergencies; he pushes the screwdriver in-between the floorboards and lifts them.

Drake looks into the concealed area with pure disgust in his face, knowing what he is being dragged into. He reaches down and picks up a black briefcase. He lays it on top of his bed; in the centre of the briefcase is a metal rectangle, with a high-tech fingerprint scanner on it. Drake keeps many secrets in his life and the secrets he keeps he wants them to stay buried. Drake puts back the floorboards, then the carpet, and moves the coffee table back.

He then gets his phone out to call Grace and the phone starts the ringing, she answers and she says to him, "Hey babe" and Drake feels reluctant to say too much, but replies with, "Hey listen, I'm going to have to postpone our date till next week. I have to go out of town for a couple of days."

Grace understands but is very confused with what is going on and replies, saying, "Yeah, that's okay, is everything all right?"

Drake has to be compartmentalised what's going on and be aware of what he says to her and replies "Just a family issue, nothing to worry about. Look I got to go, I'll call you sometime during the week."

Grace feels likes a lot is happening in such a small time and is very concerned with why Drake is being secretive, but she realises she's got to trust him, and she says, "Yeah sure, talk to you in a few days."

The phone call ends and Drake moves fast out of his room and downstairs.

Rick looks at Drake and asks, "What's in there, Drake?" knowing that it's not clothes he keeping in there, but Drake responds back saying, "Clothes."

Richard didn't push to find out what's really in there and just accepted it. They both head out the house, but before Drake goes to the car he turns around and looks at his nan with a reassuring look on his face and says, "I'll be fine, don't worry, okay?"

His nan nods her head, but with a concerned look on her, like she knows something bad is going to happen. Drake heads into the car and Rick looks at Drake and asks "You ready?"

Drake still looks concerned about what going on and what he is being dragged into, so he takes a deep breathe in and out and replies, "Sooner we do this, the sooner I can come home and get back to normal." Rick turns on the ignition, puts the car in drive and sets off for Berkshire.

Berkshire, a city of despair, misery and pain. The only place where criminals and madmen call a place like this home and also the home to infamous vigilante Nighthawk and his sidekick Redhawk. Nighthawk has been around for twenty years, taking down criminals, and Redhawk came about eight years ago. Some people think they are heroes, some people think they brought about the criminals they fight. Drake grew up here, and he has experienced first-hand what

Berkshire has to offer.

Drake and Rick come to a sign that says:

Welcome to Berkshire

Drake looks through the window at the streets of his old home; the streets look dirty and filled with criminals selling drugs and pimps selling prostitutes to make a quick buck. Drake can't help but relive the nightmares that he went through during his time here. This place is a place of horrors; everyday murder, robbery and extortion and even more happens here every day.

Drake tells his father, "This place is still a shithole why did I ever agree to come back?" and his father tries to get Drake to see the bigger picture, "Because our family is in trouble and we stand by our family no matter what."

Drake looks at his father, and in a demanding way says to his father, "Take to me see Richard's mother."

Rick rolls his eyes and tries to convince him not to see her. "Drake you won't know anything different from her that I haven't told you – there's no point."

Drake knows that's a load of bullshit, he was taught even the smallest things are helpful. Drake replies sternly "She knows more about Richard than any of us. Also, there could be something there that might help me find him – and that was one of the conditions of me coming down, so honour the agreement we have or I get the next train back." Rick knows he isn't going to change his mind, so he agrees to take him to her house.

Chapter 7

Drake and Rick pull up to a house in the slums, a location in Berkshire where people who are less fortunate than others live. The slums are run by The Scorpion Gang who is led by The Scorpion King. The house looks run down and is in need of a refurbishment. People all round the neighbourhood are either selling drugs or drugged up themselves. Drake and Rick walk through the small gate and knock on the door. The dog starts to bark loudly, and they can both hear yelling from a woman, telling the dog to be quiet. A woman with long brown hair and blue eyes wearing a flower dress answers the door.

Rick looks at the woman and says, "Hello, Ruby."

Ruby has a sarcastic tone towards Rick and says, "Hello Rick, how are you? And before you answer, I don't really care – I was just being polite."

Rick returns the favour and says "As sweet as ever, aren't you? You still shooting up on meth?"

Ruby's tone angers and she raises her hands towards Rick and says, "No I haven't, you arrogant bastard."

Drake realises that things are getting heated and changes the subject. "Miss Small my name is Drake Reynolds, I'm this arrogant bastard's son, and I'm here to find your son, Richard."

Ruby looks at Drake and has a calmer attitude towards him and says, "Can you get my son back?"

Drake looks confidently at her and says, "I will do whatever it takes to get him back. I promise."

Ruby looks at him and takes a minute to think about it, but realises she has no other choice and replies to him, "Okay. You can come in, but he stays outside."

Rick looks angered and shocked at what she says and tries to come back with fury but before he could Drake interrupts him and says, "Stay out here and before you say anything, I'm in charge during this, so you will do what I say." Rick looks at Drake sighing, and then agrees, heading back to the car whilst Drake walks in the house.

Drake walks through the hallway of Ruby's house, he notices pictures along the wall of Ruby, with a male figure with brown hair and blue eyes. He notices that there are quite a few of them, which suggests to Drake that the male figure is Richard. He also notices a really bad smell around the house, which smells like something you would find near a sewer, suggesting to Drake that this place isn't very well looked after. Drake walks into living room where he sees a poor conditioned couch and 35-inch TV.

Ruby says to Drake, "Please have a seat." Drake moves the magazines which are on the couch and sits down. Ruby offers Drake a coffee, but he declines; he just wanted to get straight to the point.

Drake realises he needs to be delicate with what he says so he chooses his words carefully and says, "Miss Small," and Ruby quickly interrupts him and says, "Ruby, please."

Drake back tracks and starts again and says, "Ruby, what I have heard from my father is that Richard is fourteen years old. He's also told me that Richard has been in trouble with drugs; now I'm guessing he's dealing not using by his age, but I want to understand why and where he could possibly be if you don't mind."

Ruby looks at Drake with concern due to not knowing why or where he is. She replies, "To be honest, Drake, I have no idea why he is doing what he is doing. For a while now I've felt like I don't know who my son is, he seems like a complete stranger. But what I do know is that he deals for the local gang The Scorpions".

Drake's facial expression isn't moved due to his past in the city. Drake knew someone growing up who dealt with drugs, so he wasn't too surprised by how Ruby is feeling. Drake looked at Ruby with sympathy and said, "I understand what you're going through. Growing up, I knew someone who dealt drugs for the Scorpions. He turned into someone I didn't recognise which is why I'm not going to let Richard get involved with them any longer."

Ruby felt some sort of comfort, knowing someone else knew how she was feeling. She looked at Drake and she said, "It's nice to know someone understands what I am going through, but I don't know where he is; he's like a stranger to me."

Drake looks at her with an idea in his head, and asks her "Does Richard have a phone?" She nods her head, confused why he asked her that. Drake follows up and asks her, "Can you write down his number, please?"

Ruby grabs a bit of paper and writes down Richard's number and asks Drake, "How is this going to help?"

Drake didn't want to disclose any information on how he is going to do it but he says, "I have a friend who can help run a lead on this. Thank you, I will be in touch soon."

Drake gets up off of the couch, and walks out of the house. Drake's phone vibrates and it's a text from:

Andrew Loid:
I know you're in town please come by the mansion so we can talk.

Drake looks at the text and ignores it instantly; he has some sort of anger towards Andrew and doesn't want anything to do with him.

Drake arrives at the car, he knocks on Rick's window and tells him, "I'm going to run down a lead, I need you to open the boot and let me get my stuff out. I'll contact you if I need you."

Rick looks confused, he was hoping they'd deal with it together and he replies, "You sure you want to go out there on your own? Like you said, you never liked Berkshire." Drake rolls his eyes at his father, like there was miscommunication between them and said, "I said I didn't like Berkshire, I never said I couldn't handle it. Just pop the boot and I'll ring you later." Rick looks at Drake, nods his head reluctantly, and pops the boot open. Drake walks to the back of the car grabs his briefcase and walks off further deep into Berkshire.

Drake arrives at an outdoor storage facility. He walks the area like he knows the place off by heart. He walks to storage area numbered 19; Drake pulls out his keys and finds the key with the number 19 on it. He puts the key in and turns it clockwise twice and then pushes up the blue door, creating a screeching sound and revealing a grey Camaro. Drake walks towards the car and opens it, and sits in the driver's seat with the briefcase on the passenger seat.

Drake looks at the briefcase and takes a deep breath in and out before putting his finger on the scanner. The case is unlocked, and Drake lifts the case open, revealing a computer with a keyboard on. He turns the computer on, revealing a logo belonging to Loid Industries on the screen. Loid Industries belongs to billionaire Andrew Loid. He logs into an account and starts to type in the number that Ruby gave him. The computer will triangulate the number's location, giving Drake the location of Richard or precisely where his phone is. Drake looked at the screen and his heart is pounding again, knowing that possibly he is going to have to go down a direction he doesn't want to go anymore. The number the computer was triangulating has found a location, a park on Victoria Road.

Drake closes the briefcase and puts it in the passenger seat. He starts the ignition of the car and puts it in drive. Drake looked in the mirror, thinking he is turning back to a life he once left behind but realising Richard is family and he needs do everything he can to help. He puts his foot on the pedal and drives out of the storage facility. He gets out of the car and pulls the blue door down and turns the lock anticlockwise to lock it. Drake then gets back in the car and starts to head to Victoria Road.

Chapter 8

Drake is parked on the Victoria Road opposite the park. He opens the glove compartment and finds a pair of binoculars. He puts the binoculars over his eyes like a pair of sunglasses, and starts to scan the area for Richard and also the men running him. Drake knows that any kids dealing drugs on the street will have some men keeping an eye on them. Drake spots Richard in the distance, with a man coming up to him. Drake knows that's a drug deal going on, and starts to look for possible targets.

He notices two men, one bald wearing a leather jacket, and one with black hair wearing jean jacket, on the right side of the park. Drake knew his only way to get Richard out of there is to pose as a customer. So, Drake puts the binoculars back in the glove compartment and gets out the car.

He heads over slowly, trying not to spook the two men. Drake finally approaches Richard, and asks him "You selling?" knowing all too well that's what he is doing.

Richard responds saying, "How much you got?"

Drake doesn't want to prolong this and says, "Richard, you don't know me okay, and you have no reason to trust me, but I am asking you to – I can get you out of this."

Richard looks confused and responds, "Look dude, I don't know who you are, but if you're not buying, move along."

Drake looks at him, getting agitated, knowing that this isn't going to go the way he thinks without being honest.

He responds, "Listen okay, your father is my father. So that makes you my brother and I am not leaving you to be some drug pusher for a lowlife gang like The Scorpions, so please come with me."

The two men realise something isn't right and come towards them. Richard replies saying, "Look, I don't want to get in trouble, please just go."

The two men appear behind them and the bald guy taps Drake on the shoulder. He asks, "What are you doing? You either buy or get lost, shit bag."

Drake looks at them noticing, their builds, trying to end this peacefully and says, "Listen, he is not selling anymore drugs for you or your Scorpion King. He leaves with me."

The two men start laughing at him and the guy in jean jacket tells him, "Dude, piss off before we knock your pretty face in."

Drake looks at them and starts to say, "Listen he's leaving with—" and the guy in the jean jacket hits Drake in the face, knocking him down to the floor.

Drake now knows there's no reasoning with them and gets back up. The guy in the in the jean jacket strikes at Drake again, but before he could make contact, Drake blocks the punch and grabs his wrist and twists it and breaks it. The guy in the leather jacket tries to strike Drake multiple times, but he blocks all them. Drake finds an opening and punches the guy in stomach, then ducks underneath another punch the guy threw at him. He quickly lands a jab in his ribs and gets behind the guy and kicks him in the back of legs, breaking one of them. Then he finally lands one more punch in the face, knocking one of his opponents out cold.

The second guy, whose wrist Drake broke, comes charging at Drake, trying to punch him in the face. Drake grabs the guy's arm and lifts his body up, with his legs wrapped around the guy's neck. He puts all his weight into his legs and pulls the guy to floor, and lands one last blow to the face, knocking his final opponent out.

Drake grabs Richard and tells him "We're going."

Richard follows Drake towards the car. Drake says, "Get in." They both rush into the car and Drake speeds off in a hurry.

Drake and Richard are in the car, speeding down the streets like two hooligans on a joy ride. Drake didn't want it to go down the way it did. He thought he could slip in get his brother and get out without causing a fuss, but he realised it wasn't an option. Richard is sat in the passenger seat, shaking after what just happened. Drake didn't know what to say to him, but he knew it was the right thing to do.

Drake pulls out a bottle of water from the side door and hands it to Richard. He says, "Have some water, it will help with the shock."

Richard just sits there and looks through the window, contemplating if this is reality or a dream. Drake realised he's not going to reach Richard at the moment, so he decides to take command.

Drake breathes in and out then he says, "Look I'm going to put you somewhere safe whilst I deal with this. You're going to be fine."

Richard doesn't feel any comfort in what he said, and he then replies, "This would've never happened if you didn't interfere. Now I am dead, thanks to you". Drake doesn't know what to say to him; it wasn't long ago when Drake blamed someone for his misfortunes.

Drake pulls up to an apartment building on Reacher Avenue, the area is quite posh and very expensive, and something Drake couldn't afford alone.

Richard steps out the car, and is confused why they are in the posh part of the city and says, "Why are we here?"

Drake turns off the ignition and gets out the car. He looks at Richard and tells him, "It's a safe place, where we can remain hidden from The Scorpions."

They head to the front door where there is a keypad with a five-digit code to enter. Drake looks at the keypad and enters the code – 52652. The door buzzes like a bee and he opens it. In the hallway, there is an elevator at the end of the room. Along the hallway, there is a picture of a historical boat.

Drake and Richard walk along the corridor and arrive at the elevator, but there is retinal scan to open the lift. Drake hopes that the owner hasn't taken his scan out of the database. Suddenly the camera next to the elevator turns on and points at Drake. He puts his eyes close the scanner so that it can read his eyes, and suddenly the scanners database blinked red and comes back saying, 'Access Failed'.

Drake noticed the camera pointing at him and he instantly knows who is watching. He says to the camera, "Let me in," and nothing happens.

So Drake continues, "Let me in, you son of a bitch, you owe me." Still nothing happens.

Drake makes an offer. "Look if you open this door, I'll

come to see you when I'm finished, on my mother's memory."

Suddenly the elevator doors open quickly. Richard is confused at who Drake is talking to and asks, "Who were you talking to?"

Drake looks at the camera and nods, and the heads into the elevator. He replies saying, "None of your business."

There are five levels on the elevator pad. The fifth floor is the penthouse, which is where Drake is heading. He pushes the fifth floor, and the doors close. The last time Drake was here he was bleeding in the bathtub – there weren't many fond memories for Drake here.

The doors open and suddenly an expensive fantasy appears, but it's not a fantasy. Richard walks in, surprised at how expensive this place is and how beautiful the architecture is of the place.

He is stunned and asks, "How the hell can you afford a place like this?"

Drake didn't want him knowing too much about his life, but replies saying, "It was given to me by someone."

Drake activates the security system that is in place, and says to Richard, "The rooms are deadlocked, the windows are bulletproof, and the entrances can't be accessed without a code and Retinal scan. This place is one hundred percent safe, no-one will get you here."

Richard looks a little bit more relaxed seeing all the security that's in place and asks Drake, "So what now?"

Drake didn't want say too much but replies with, "I am going to locate the Scorpion King and get him to cut you out of the gang permanently."

Richard looks at him with not a lot of faith and says,

"You think it's going to be that easy? No-one has even seen the guy, and even if you find him he will kill you and then come after me, he will never let me go."

Drake tries to show Richard he's tougher than he thinks.

"I'm more persuasive than you think. Anyway, I need to know why, 'cause I don't understand why someone like you would get involved with The Scorpions."

Richard looks at Drake, knowing he will have to come clean sooner or later and replies, "As you're probably aware, I don't come from much and my mother she has debt, a lot more then she lets on, I kept seeing her struggle, day in, day out – it was hard. So one day, I saw some kids selling drugs, and I asked them how much they made. It was a lot, and I saw the money in the bag that they had next to them so I distracted them and took the bag and I gave it to my mother."

Drake knew where this was leading and felt bad for him and replied with sympathy. "Let me guess; they found out it was you and they didn't take it too well."

Richard looks at Drake with surprise that he understands. He replies, "Something like that. One of the people that work for the king said to me that he doesn't respond well to people stealing from him, so he told me I have to work off my debt by selling his drugs."

Drake was curious how much Richard owed and asked, "How much do you owe them?"

Richard looked worried, but replied "£20,000."

Drake looks at Richard and asked him, "Where do you meet the guys to get the drugs?"

Richard instantly replies. "An apartment building on Kyle Street, but its heavily protected."

Drake wasn't too concerned with that fact and replies, "I'm not worried about that. Okay, stay here. I'll handle this."

Drake walks towards elevator doors and pulls out his phone, looks for Andrew Loid on his contacts and dials it.

Suddenly a British voice appears on the other end and says, "I've been expecting your call."

Drake wasn't really concerned at what Andrew was saying and replies, "Look I'm not calling for that, but I do intend to keep our agreement."

Andrew knew exactly why he was calling. "Yeah, I know you're calling for £20,000 your brother owes The Scorpions."

Drake was instantly enraged and replies, "You were eavesdropping on my conversation. Look, it doesn't matter – will you lend me the £20,000 or not?"

Andrew knew he wasn't going to get a pleasant conversation from Drake at this time, but replies, "Well, 'lend' means I'll end up getting it back. So no, I won't lend it to you but I'll give you £25,000 so that they feel they're gaining something, but on the condition after this you keep your word and come by the mansion. I have something we need to discuss."

Drake felt making a deal with Andrew was like making a deal with the devil but he had no choice. "You always have something to say, but fine. You give me the money, and I'll stay true to my word and come by."

Andrew believes his words are genuine and directs Drake to the cash. He says, "Go to the room on the bottom floor and then enter the code 68901 on the keypad. once you're there, you will see a safe. Your finger print will work on it, the cash is in there. I'll see you soon."

Drake follows the instructions to the letter and opens the safe. He finds the cash he needs, but also something odd. There is white envelope with Andrew's name on it, and the envelope looks old. He picks up the envelope and opens it up, revealing a photo of two people. Drake is shocked – it is Andrew and Drake's Mother.

Chapter 9

Drake is driving to Kyle Street. Kyle Street is heavily populated with drug dealers, drug users and from the research that Drake did a few years ago, it is, or maybe was, a central location for The Scorpions.

Drake is still shocked and confused at why Andrew is in a photo with his mother. His head is spinning with theories, but he realised that he needs to stay focused on what is at hand.

Drake pulls up to the apartment block and as Drake thought; its crawling with Scorpions, Drake knew he needed to be smart if he is to make it out alive. Drake pulls out the cash Andrew gave him from the glove compartment, and also pulls a knife from the compartment as well. He gets out of his car and puts the knife in-between his trousers and puts the cash in his jacket pocket.

Drake gets a call on his phone from Grace. Before Drake went in, his takes the call by his car.

He says, "Hey, babe. Listen, it's not a good time can I call you later?"

Grace is concerned and was very worried about Drake saying, "I know you're probably busy but I am very worried about you. Last time we spoke, you were very secretive, I just wanted to make sure you are all right."

Drake felt very comforted, knowing someone not related to him cares about him a lot. He didn't want to tell her anything about what's going on so he reassured her instead.

"Look babe, I'm all right. Just got a lot on at the moment. I got to go, but when I'm back me and you can spend a lovely meal together under the sunset. How does that sound?"

Grace didn't feel any less worried, but knew she couldn't push, so she just said, "Okay, as long as you're safe, that's all that matters. We will talk soon."

Drake made a quick reply, "Yeah, talk soon. Bye now." He hangs up and gets his mind back in the game.

Drake looks at the apartment building and takes a deep breath in and out, knowing things could go sideways easily. He walks towards the entrance of the apartment building, and noticed there are three guys wearing hoodies sitting on the steps; this area felt like something out of a zombie movie with all the people loitering around.

Drake goes up to them and says, "I want to meet your boss."

The men look at Drake and laugh at him like he is a piece of dirt on their shoes. Drake pulls out the money from his jacket pocket and says, "I want to make a deal with him."

The men look at each other, deciding whether to let him up there or not. Then one of the men nods his head to the side, indicting for him to follow. Drake follows the men up the apartment building; the smell is the stench of death, and all Drake can see is people with knives and guns along the building.

Drake approaches a door, which the men lead him to.

The men leave and Drake knocks on the door loudly. A slider on the door opens, showing a man with green eyes, who says, "What do you want?"

Drake remains strong and says, "I'm here to do business with your boss." He pulls out the cash showing a sign of good faith.

Ten seconds later the door opens. Drake walks in and slowly manoeuvres between rooms seeing, woman and men drugged up and hearing loud music. Drake is analysing the apartment trying to find key ways to leave if things go wrong. The deeper Drake goes into the apartment, the louder the music gets. Drake is brought to a room – the man who led him there halts him, and the man goes into the room and announces his presence.

Drake feels anxious and his heart starts to pound, he takes a deep breath in and out, and suddenly the door opens. Drake walks into the room – there's two couches on the side, with desk in the back with a load of cocaine and meth on it. There is also a guy in a chair facing the wall.

The guy starts to talk to Drake and says, "So you have come here to make a deal – what kind of deal do you have to offer?"

Drake recognises that voice but he can't contemplate that it's who he thinks it is. The guy turns around; he is wearing a grey suit and has short brown hair and blue eyes and says, "Drake Reynolds, what brings you here?"

Drake replies in shock saying, "Adam."

Drake is shocked about who is siting opposite him, Adam Langford his best friend back when he was in secondary school. Adam was a drug user turned drug dealer back in the day. Drake tried everything he could to get through to him, but nothing helped.

Drake asks Adam, "How is this possible? Last time I saw you, you were a drug dealer."

Adam's facial expression turn to smugness, and says to Drake, "You see, that's how it all starts; you start small and you work your way up."

Drake can't believe how low his old friend has fallen and says, "Before the drugs, you used to be a good person, you used to care about people and then one bad day and your life has turned to shit – how the mighty have fallen."

Adam looks a Drake with a gaze and says, "Fallen, mate? I've never felt higher. I've made something of myself – what have you done?"

Drake is angered with what Adam is saying, and he replies to him with honesty, "At least I haven't sold my soul. Look if you're high up, then you can get me a meeting with The Scorpion King."

Adam laughs at Drake and tells him a secret that will stun him.

"Oh my, you still are thick, aren't you? I can't pass a message on to myself. You see, Drake, I am the Scorpion King."

Drake was shocked at what he heard; he knew the only way he got that title was by killing people. He looks at Adam with disgust and says, "That's impossible. You're not capable of murder. Even if you are, the Scorpion King, the Nighthawk would've stopped you, because he would've seen weakness in the organisation and used that to take you down."

Adam looks at Drake, laughing, having no care in the world for Nighthawk, and says, "Nighthawk? Don't make me laugh. He's far too busy fighting the Crow and the Mob to come after me. Anyway, enough with this – why are you here?"

Drake knows he is not going to be able to reason with Adam, so he is just going to have to be direct and replies, "Richard Small. I know he owes you £20,000 and I'm here to pay off his debt. In return, I want him out of The Scorpions and to never be bothered again." Drake throws the money on the desk and tried to remain in control of the situation.

Adam is intrigued and replies, "Wait. I had two men of mine attacked earlier today by someone trying to take Richard. Is that just a coincidence."

Drake's temper rises, but remains in control to say, "Do we have an agreement?"

Adam walks rounds the desk and says to Drake, "The thing is, Drake, I was never going to let him go. He stole from me, and today he betrayed me, so now he's dead."

Drake's temper rises even further and moves forward towards Adam and replies, "I won't let that happen, so I'm going make you another offer. Take the money and leave Richard alone, or I break everything fucking bone your body."

One of the men behind Drake points a gun to Drake's head and Adam starts to get angry and says, "You think you can come in here and threaten me? Just for that I'm going to kill you, then I'm going kill Richard and after that, just to set an example, I'm going after his mother, and I am going to do shit to her that would even make the devil run in terror. Shoot him."

Drake knew he had to act fast, so he moved backwards so he could feel the gun on the back of his head. He ducked and turned around to face the man but before he stopped, he grabbed his gun. The man starting shooting, and there were two other men besides Adam in the room. Drake moved the gun whilst it was shooting in the direction of the other guy's leg and then quickly disarmed the guy with the gun. He kicked the second guy who was heading towards him, and then pulled out the knife from his trousers.

He slashes the guy he disarmed in the ribs, then grabbed his arm and slashed a nerve in his wrist, stopping him from opening the hand. He then did a high kick to his face knocking him out cold. He then turned his attention to the guy he kicked, he put the knife back in his trousers, and engaged in hand-to-hand combat. They guy attempted to hit Drake in the face but he quickly blocked, and then kneed the guy in the stomach and hit him in the face as hard he could, knocking him out.

Drake turns his attention to Adam. He grabs Adam's head and slams it on his desk, and to show he wasn't joking around, grabs the knife again and puts it through Adam's hand.

Adam is screaming in pain and Drake is still holding the knife, which is in Adam's hand and he says, "Now let's start again. Take the money and stay away from Richard."

Drake twists the knife making Adam scream in agony.

Adam yells, "Okay okay! you have a deal, I won't make a move on him." Drake lets go of the knife and leaves the room. A man runs into the room checking, on his boss. He says, "Boss, you all right?"

Adam takes the knife out of his hand and says, "I want you to follow him. He will lead you to Richard. Bring me the boy and then kill Drake Reynolds."

Chapter 10

Drake is in the car, driving back to the safe house, he is shaken to his core at what he did. He didn't know he was capable of that anymore, but he soon realises there was no other choice, that he had to show true dominance in that situation. Drake instructs the car to call Ruby. Whilst it was ringing, he didn't know what he was going to say to her, and then the call connects.

Ruby says, "Hello, who is this?" Drake took a moment before responding and says, "Hi Ruby, it's Drake. I've managed to get Richard away from The Scorpions; whatever hold they have over him is now gone."

Ruby is surprised by what she's hearing. Through the phone, Drake can hear that she's getting emotional.

She replies, "OMG, how did you manage to do that?"

Drake didn't want to tell her how it happened, so he just stated, "It doesn't matter. What matters now is that he is safe. Come pick him up at Reacher Avenue, he will be waiting outside." Ruby is so overwhelmed with emotion that she finally has her son back. She doesn't know what more to say then, "I'm on my way now. Thank you, Drake." Drake didn't feel like he deserved that thank you – if only she knew how he had got Richard back.

But he replies with, "You don't need to thank me,". The call gets disconnected, and Drake feels like he gave into the darkness that he was fighting these last three years.

Drake arrives back at the safe house, and he walks in on Richard watching the news of Nighthawk saving the mayor from Dr Tarantula. Drake couldn't stand to hear anything about Nighthawk and walks over to the remote and turns it off.

Richard shouts, "Hey I was watching that" in frustration.

Drake starts to be direct and tells him, "You get to go home, Richard, I've dealt with The Scorpions. Your debt with them has been expunged, you're free."

Richard can't believe what he is hearing, He knows too well what The Scorpions are like and finds it hard to believe that they just let him go so easily.

Richard asks, "How did you get them to clear my debt?"

Drake knew he had to say something, like what he told his mother to give reassurance, so he said, "I was very persuasive, and I also gave them the money you owe. Don't ask how just accept that its over."

Richard didn't want to push so he says to Drake, "Thank you."

Drake and Richard move to the elevator and Drake replies, "Don't mention it, just stay away from the drugs business. It's a nasty place to be. Promise me".

Richard didn't need time to think and just replied, saying, "I promise."

They both get in the elevator and Drake pushes the button for ground floor, they both look at each other, finally happy that the situation is over. The elevator closes and they both head down.

Drake and Richard walk through the hallway on the ground floor, and they see Ruby waiting outside for her son. Richard runs in joy to his mother, pushing the door open like he had the strength of ten men and leapt into her arms.

Ruby starts to cry; they are tears of happiness and she asks him, "Are you all right, my boy?"

Richard reassures his mother by saying, "I'm fine, Mum – it was all thanks to Drake."

Drake appears next to them. Ruby gave Drake a hug whilst saying, "Thank you. This means a lot to me and my son, I don't know how I could repay you."

Drake never did what he did for recognition or for reward, he did it because it was right;

He says, "No repayment necessary. Richard is family and so are you, so if there is anything you need in the future, you give me a call."

Richard and Ruby start to walk across the street. Suddenly a car swerves around the corner and brakes heavily. Four men wearing balaclavas, strapped with AK47s, come out of the car. Drake rushes to Richard and Ruby as fast as he can. The men start to open fire on them.

Drake grabs Ruby and pushes her behind the car, Drake can't reach Richard, but he shouted, "Get to cover!"

Drake notices someone coming around the corner of the car he and Ruby are behind and tells Ruby, "Stay down and don't move until I say so."

As soon as he sees the foot of the guy, he rushes towards him and grabbing the gun. He manages to flip the man to the floor and takes the gun off him and hits him in the face to knock him out, and quickly opens fire on the men shooting.

Drake suddenly hears Richard crying out for help, but the men buddle him into the car. Drake is trying to aim for the tyres, but they speed off, like a bolt of lightning.

Ruby cries out Richard's name. Drake is shocked that Adam had backed out of the agreement and hired men to take Richard.

Ruby looks at Drake with full of rage and says to him, "You told me you fixed this, you said he was safe!"

Drake didn't know what to say at first, and then states, "I'll get him back."

Ruby is very emotional and is confused with what Drake can do to fix this and responds, "What are you going to do?"

Drake doesn't answer but notices the guy on the floor. Drake drags the guy into the building and leans him against the wall. Ruby remains outside, not knowing what to do next.

Drake needed information from the unconscious man, fast. He notices a water fountain and sees a bucket on the other side of the room. Drake goes to fill the bucket up with water. He heads back to the guy but before he throws the water, he notices a knife and takes it, with the intent on using it. Drake knew now he had to become the person he was before.

Drake grabs the bucket and throws it over the guy, a sudden shock that woke the guy instantly, and he is confused as to what's going on. Drake looks at the guy and takes his balaclava off, his facial expression is full of rage and demands to know where his brother is.

The guy says, "You're not getting shit out of me, you think you scare me more than the King himself – you're way out of your depth."

Drake looks at him and he pulls the knife out of its cover and says, "You don't know what I am capable of – let me show you."

Drake stabs the knife into the guy's leg. The guy is screaming in pain, yelling, "You son of a bitch!"

Drake twists the knife to create pain for the guy, to show him who is in charge, and says in an intimidating way, "Now I can twist knife ever so slightly, so I can hit an artery and make you bleed out. Now tell me where Richard is."

The guy looks at him, now knowing he means business and is scared of him and says, "Fine – their taking him to an old meat factory on Jameson Street. God, stop please."

Drake takes the knife out of the guy and grabs his balaclava and tells him, "Apply pressure, the ambulance will be here soon."

Drake runs out the building and tells Ruby, "Call an ambulance for the guy in there. I've kept the door open so they can get in."

Ruby is confused about what's going on and asks, "Where you going?"

Drake runs to his car and opens the door, but before he gets in, he says, "I'm getting Richard back." He gets in the car, turns the ignition on and drives off, full speed ahead.

Drake knew he had to make a stop first, so he went to a derelict building site, owned by Loid Industries. Drake drives his car to a dead end, but the dead end is more than what it seems. Drake opened the glove compartment where there is a remote. He grabbed it and aimed it at the wall ahead. Suddenly the floor began to sink – creating a secret entrance for Drake to go down. Drake is not too pleased with what is about to happen and is also not too pleased at where he is about to go, but he knows there is no other way.

Drake drives down the ramp into the secret entrance, lights turning on while he was driving. He finally reached the end of the road. Drake took a deep breath in and out and then steps out the car and shouts "ON!"

Suddenly, everything is turning on, and you can see a massive open space with a big computer in the centre with a medical wing on it sides. There is also an armoury for all the gear, and the last thing to turn on was the capsule.

Drake stood in front of that capsule, waiting for it turn on and eventually it did, revealing the secret Drake has been hiding from his friends, his family and the love of his life.

The capsule revealed a black suit with red lining, with a red hawk for a symbol on the right of his chest, and a red mask with hawk ears extending from the sides. Drake's big secret is revealed – Drake was the superhero Redhawk, side kick to Nighthawk. Drake looks at the costume with his heart pounding through his chest, and says, "Hello, old friend."

Chapter 11

Drake started being Redhawk when he was twelve years old, in 2012, on the dark and gritty streets of Berkshire.

Nighthawk saw Drake around the slums, depressed, alone and angry at the world. Nighthawk noticed that Drake was being bullied a lot. It turns out Nighthawk had gone to Drake's school to make a donation to improve the technology department, and he witnessed how much Drake was suffering by the hands of bullies. No-one noticed him; he came without wearing his mask.

One night, Nighthawk was on patrol. He had recently just taken down a serial killer who cut peoples head's off and stuck them on pikes. Berkshire was like that; people outside the city said it's a hell of its own making.

On that night, Drake saw this woman being dragged into an ally way. Drake couldn't stand by when someone was in trouble, so he did what he thought was right and intervened. Drake didn't have any fighting experience but couldn't stand by and watch.

Drake got his ass kicked and the guy was going to kill him but suddenly a guy dropped down and beat the guy up. Nighthawk seeing Drake put his life on the line for someone else gave Nighthawk the idea to take him under his wing and train him to be stronger.

Throughout the years, Nighthawk and Redhawk fought to

keep the streets free from criminals and super criminals. In the last couple of years, Nighthawk and Drake started to be at odds and ended up drifting apart. Drake believed his methods were too brutal and that Nighthawk only saw the world as black and white. So, when Drake was told by his mother that they were going to move to Devon, Drake knew this was a chance to get away from the life. Nighthawk went solo again, he took it personally when Drake left, and Drake hadn't seen him since.

As Drake looked at his suit for the first time in ages, he felt like he knew he would end up back where he started before he left.

He believed that Redhawk was just a means to an end. He believed that if he continued being Redhawk, he would end up six feet under. As a kid, Drake wanted to be a superhero; he admired what Nighthawk did and stood for, but from first-hand experience, Drake knew what kind of life he was leading into. A life Drake has been trying to stay away from since he left.

Drake walked over to the big computer and took a seat. The computer is almost the size of a cinema screen; superheroes tend to overcompensate with their gear. Drake logs into the computer to access the Loid Industries satellite, he wants to use the satellite to get thermal imaging on the location where Richard is held. Thermal imaging will determine how many heat signatures are in the building. The heat signatures will then show how many people are in the building and where they're based, giving Drake the tactical advantage. Drake analysed the screen, revealing three men on the top floor and three men, not including

Richard are on the bottom floor. Drake knew the best tactical advantage was to enter from the roof, Drake has the tools to do so.

Drake walks over to the capsule holding his suit. He looks at it, thinking it's a bad reflection of him. But he knows he hasn't got another way of handling this. He believes he has to let the darkness in to save his brother.

Drake opens the glass door, and removes the black and red trousers. He puts the trousers on one leg at a time, then slowly moves to the armoured chest plates with built in Kevlar. Then he puts on the gloves with built in knuckledusters for extra power.

Drake thinks to himself, "The suit fits perfectly," and finally he puts the mask on, with built-in Kevlar and voice modulator, to disguise his voice. The lens has a built-in computer, giving Drake the ability to use thermal imaging in the field. It also has communication features built in as well but there is no-one he needed to communicate with.

Drake then walks over to the armoury to get his weapons he used to use all the time. Drake grabs his utility belt with a holster on the side, clipping it around his waist. He then picks up a red crossbow with a built-in grapple gun, He looks at it like it's an instrument that hasn't been played in a while. Drake used to have a compulsion to use the weapon, just like he used to have a compulsion to be Redhawk, it was like he need to be him and to use the weapon to make a difference. Now he can't stand the sight of it.

Drake leaves the armoury and heads to where he parked his car, but he realises there is a faster way to get to where he needs to be. He walks over to an object with a sheet over it. He pulls off the sheet, revealing a red and black motorcycle. He pulls his hand along the bike stroking it like it's a pet. This vehicle is the only thing from Drake's superhero days that he missed and appreciated. Drake sat on the bike, turns on the ignition and revs the engine a few times, and then sets out back through the secret passageway back onto the streets of Berkshire.

Redhawk arrives at meat factory where Adam, aka the Scorpion King, is holding his brother. He knows he needs to get to the roof; he reaches for his crossbow. The curved edges of the crossbow pop out, he changes the crossbow into the grapple by pushing a button on the side, loading an arrow attached to a strong metal cable that can hold Redhawk's weight.

He aims crossbow at the edge of the building. He fires the arrow; the arrow moves fast, like a shooting star. The arrow embeds itself into the wall; Redhawk tugs at the cable to make sure its strong and tight. The crossbow has an accelerator built in to allow Redhawk to accelerate upwards towards the arrow, to get him to high places. Redhawk zips through the air like a bullet, with the speed he's going Redhawk will go beyond the arrow to allow him to reach edge without climbing. He lands on the edge with two feet and the arrow releases zipping back into the crossbow. Redhawk changes the crossbow back to its normal function, shooting regular arrows.

Redhawk notices a door that leads into the factory. But before he goes in, he scans the building for heat signatures to see where they are. He sees that there is three men on either side of the walkways on the top floor. Redhawk knows his tactical approach would need to be taking the three of them out first, quietly, before going for the rest. He heads into the building via the door.

Redhawk hides behind the doorway and leans out to see what he can see, noticing one strapped with an AK47. He knows he needs to take them out quietly, so he has to get his attention. Knowing that they are all spaced out means it will be easy to do so.

Redhawk sees a bit of metal on the floor and throws it through the doorway. The guy reacts jittery, he slowly walks towards the doorway, with his gun raised. Redhawk has to time this perfectly, and takes a deep breath in and out. The guy's foot is in the doorway; Redhawk quickly grabs the guy and the gun and spins him behind the door. He lands hard strike on the guy, hitting his head on floor, He knocks him unconscious. Redhawk has always been taught never to kill and has been taught only non-lethal fighting styles.

Redhawk quickly rushes into the doorway and notices a guy in the middle of the walkway. The tactic he used last time isn't going to work this time – he needs to find another way to take him down. He notices a bit of scaffolding that edged out from the ceiling; it will hold his weight.

Redhawk switches his crossbow back to a grapple, and fires above the scaffolding. He launches himself without being seen and crouches. He knows he can't take him out until the other guy is further away from him. He turns his crossbow back to its normal function again, he aims the arrow at the other end the walkway and fires the arrow. They guy moved towards the sound, on alert. Now that the guy is further away, Redhawk can now drop down on the guy below him. He falls down landing on top of the guy;

the fall alone doesn't knock him out so Redhawk rolls back to his feet and punches him in the back of the head, knocking him out.

Redhawk knows the guy is too far away to get close without being seen. So, he has to move fast. Whilst the guy is still looking the other way, he runs straight at him, the guy turns around. Redhawk quickly shoots an arrow in the guy's shoulder, for an instant he is distracted and in pain. Redhawk quickly jumps into the air and knees the guy in the face. He also lands several punches in the stomach and then finally uses an uppercut to knock him out cold.

Redhawk managed to take them all out without alerting the guys below. He looks over the edge, seeing two men and Adam; he also sees Richard, dangling above a meat grinder. Redhawk's anger grows, but he has to stay level-headed to get Richard back safe. He can hear what Adam is saying to Richard.

Adam says, "So you think you can betray me? After my generosity of not killing you for stealing from me."

Richard cries out, saying, "Please I'm sorry I didn't want to go it just happened so fast my brother he found me and told me he would get me out, please I'm sorry!"

Adam is surprised to learn that Richard is Drake's brother. He replies, "Wait, your Drake's brother? Oh god, we have hit the gold mine. Now, when I kill you, it's going to make him suffer. Hit the switch; let's see what he had for lunch."

Richard cries out, "No, please no!" The guy turns on the machine and presses the button to lower Richard in. Redhawk has to act quickly and remembers he has a pocket emp in his utility belt. He takes it out and hits the button in the middle. Suddenly, all the lights and machines stopped working.

Adam says, "What the hell is going on? What happened to the lights?"

Redhawk shouts, with his voice sounding deeper and more electronic – like a robot – due to the voice modulator. "GET AWAY FROM HIM."

Instantly the guys raise their guns to the walkway. They hear swooshing in the distance and they open fire in a panic.

One of the guys say, "It's Nighthawk, we don't stand a chance."

Adam gets angry and says to his men, "Shoot anything that moves! Do you understand me?"

Redhawk uses his grapple from his crossbow and shoots it at one of the guy's legs, he accelerates up into the darkness, screaming. Redhawk sees his face and punches him knocking him out cold. He wraps the cable around the walkway banisters. Then he moves to another location. He sees the two guys below and jumps down, still remaining in the darkness.

One of the guys is close enough for Redhawk to grab, so he grabs him and brings him back into the darkness and all Adam and the other guy can hear is screaming.

Adam pulls out a Glock pistol from his jacket pocket and tells the guy, "Fire, you dipshit."

The guy open fires where his partner was dragged into the darkness and then says, "I think he is dead."

Suddenly, he hears a voice behind him, saying in a sinister way, "You thought wrong."

The guy turns around but before he could raise his gun Redhawk took the gun and threw it away, punched him on the nose, and then did a roundhouse kick to his face, resulting in the guy on the floor, unconscious.

Adam looks at Redhawk, surprised at who he sees before him and says, "I thought you died."

Redhawk is extremely angry and says, "You were wrong. Now are you going to fight me like a man, or shoot me like a pussy?"

Adam looks at him succumbing, to peer pressure and drops the gun, replying, "I don't need a gun to take you down."

Suddenly, they manoeuvre towards one another. Adam throws punches towards Redhawk's face but they result to no effect, due to him blocking. Redhawk responds with harder punches to his face, the manoeuvring down towards the stomach, landing some body shots. Redhawk then kicks Adam back, Redhawk is out for blood. Adam is panting and bleeding down his face, due to the cuts that Redhawk caused.

Adam says, "Is that all you got? Do you know who I am?"

Redhawk looks at him thinking, he is a disgrace to what humanity is meant to be. He replies. "A jumped-up little shit who thinks he's a hard man because he carries a gun and give orders. All you are is just like an demon doing the devil's work, and let me tell you something I've gone up against real demons and you don't even compare."

Adam looks at him and tries to swing at Redhawk, but he dodges then he knees him in the stomach, resulting in him falling to the floor. Redhawk pulls out his crossbow and shoots him in the leg.

Adam screams out in pain and says, "You cunt, I'll kill

you!"

Redhawk points his crossbow at Adam's face and has a surge of anger running through him and says, "You pray on innocent children to do your work and you kill to get your way. The drug you spread around the slums kills parents and children."

Adam looks at him, testing Redhawk's humanity. "Then kill me, go on do it. You know if you don't, I will come after you and I will kill you, then I'll come after him and kill him and his family." Redhawk's crossbow is shaking because he wants to kill him for all the pain he has inflicted on others and he wants to protect his brother.

But he remembers what his mother said "You are a good person and you know what's right and what's wrong. You are a light bringer."

He looks at Adam and says, "I'm not you. I will never take a life, because I appreciate what life gives and you're going to rot in prison for what you have done and you won't hurt anyone again." He lowers the crossbow and instead grabs Adam, drags him to a metal pipe and pulls out handcuffs and cuffs him to it.

Redhawk runs over to the control system and reaches for the emp he has and turns it off. He uses the control system to lower Richard on the floor safely. He takes an arrow out of his crossbow and uses it to cut the rope that is holding Richard's hands together. Richard's facial expression turns from scared to shocked that he survived, and that Redhawk saved him.

Redhawk looks at Richard and says, "You're safe now, go outside and call the police."

Richard is confused on how he got involved and asks

"How did you know I was in trouble?"

Redhawk can't tell Richard who he is, because he would be in more danger but he twists the truth and says, "Your brother told me what happened – now go." Redhawk moves back to the walkways, watching over Adam and his crew until police arrive.

Ten mins later, Redhawk hears police sirens and red and blue light hit the glass windows reflecting in the building. Police officers come in with guns, screaming, "Police! Put your hands in the air!"

The men look at Adam, handcuffed to the pipe and see the note on his body left by Redhawk: 'I am Adam Langford and I am the Scorpion King. Go to the Kyle Street apartment building, top floor to see my crimes.'

The cops look at this and are confused as to who did this. The cops read Adam his rights and then gets taken away and put into a police car.

Redhawk leaves the building, knowing everyone is safe. Suddenly, he gets a call from Grace on his phone.

He turns off his modulator and answers, "Hey, babe. Before you say anything, I'm fine I've managed to deal with the family issue." Grace is relieved to know everything is all right and says, "I'm glad to hear that, hun – so does that mean you're coming back?"

Drake is glad to hear from her, but he has to do one more thing which he has to be honest with her about, but not go into detail, because he doesn't think she would understand.

He says, "Yes I will be back, but I have to do one more thing before I leave. Nothing important, just something I have been putting off for a while. Book a table for us at that fancy restaurant you like – I owe you a date. See you soon."

He hangs up the phone. He heads back to the bunker to put all his gear away. It's been a long night and he has no intention of doing a patrol like he used to.

Chapter 12

It's the next day after Richard's terrible ordeal. Drake has driven to the police station to pick up Richard and Ruby. He has parked opposite the station so that they can find him. Drake stands next to his car, leaning against it.

Drake looks like his daydreaming because he is lost in thought. He feels partly responsible for how the situation played out. Drake starts to think that if he handled it better in the first place, Richard may never have been in danger. Drake looks at his surroundings watching criminals be brought into the station and victims come out; he can tell the difference because criminal tend to leave with a smile on their faces thinking they got away with it, whilst victims tend to be in tears. Drake starts to think if being Redhawk was making a difference or not.

Drake notices Richard and Ruby and raises his hand to signal them over. Richard looks and feels traumatised, but also shows signs of relief, knowing it's over.

Richard asks "What you doing here?"

Drake wanted to be honest with him and he replies "I feel partly responsible for what happened to you and I thought giving you a lift home was the least I can do. I know it doesn't fix what happened, but it's the first step."

Richard looks at Drake with a smile showing that he doesn't blame him.

"It's fine, dude. Look, it wasn't your fault. You helped

me get free, so I want to thank you."

Drake breathes a sigh of relief, knowing his brother doesn't blame him. Drake opens the door to his car; he pushes forward the seat to let Richard in. Drake looks at Richard and moves his head to the side, telling him to get in. Ruby walks round the other side of the car and gets in the front passenger seat. Drake looks at the police station still reminiscing on his past work as Redhawk. Drake feels even though he hated the brutality and despair that the job brought, he still feels he made a difference in the city.

Ruby notices Drake staring at the police station and she asks him, "Are you all right, Drake?"

Drake quickly turns around and gets in the car and replies, "Yes sorry – just memories that's all. You ready to go home?"

Ruby and Richard both look at each other, noticing they're having the same thought and they say in unison, "Yes." Drake turns the car on and sets the car in drive and he says, "Home it is," he drives them both home.

Drake pulls in to Ruby and Richard's house and Ruby notices Rick's car out front.

Ruby is surprised that he is here. She asks Drake, "What's he doing here?"

Drake knew that he was worried about Richard, so he replies, "I told him I'm bringing you guys home. Look, I know you believe he doesn't have any right to be here. I agree he hasn't been around, but if I was a parent, I would want to know my child is all right."

Ruby rolls her eyes, but she knows deep down that Drake is right, she takes a deep breath in and out and gets out the car.

She walks towards him whilst Drake and Richard wait in the car.

Rick panics and starts to say what's on his mind. "Listen I know I'm the last person you want to talk to, but I just wanted see him to know he is all right."

Ruby notices the worry and love in Rick's eyes something she thought he was incapable of feeling. She looks at him with compassion and says, "Look. Are you my favourite person in the world? No. Are you his father though? Yes, and if I was in your shoes, I would want to see my child. But he needs someone stable, not someone who's in and out of his life. Now if you're capable of that, then I'll allow you to see him, but if you're not, you can leave now."

Rick knows he hasn't been the best and realises he needs to be better and he says, "I won't let him down again I promise."

Ruby signals Drake to come over. Drake gets out the car and helps Richard out as well. Richard is confused and asks Drake, "What's going on?"

Drake walks him over and says, "You're about to meet your father." Richard starts to get anxious; his heart is pounding, and he starts to sweat. Ruby grabs Richard by the hand to show him everything is all right.

She says, "Richard I would like to introduce you to your father."

Rick puts out his hand to share pleasantries. He feels nervous, thinking his son might reject him, but he says, "Hello Richard. My name's Rick. I'm your dad."

There's a pause for a couple of seconds; tensions are high, but Richard breaks the tension by exchanging pleasantries back by shaking his father's hand, and says, "Hey, Dad. It's good to finally meet you."

Ruby says, "Let's all go inside, can't stay out here all day."

Drake appreciates the offer but he has a promise to keep. He says, "I would love to, but I have to start heading back, but thank you."

He looks at Richard and puts an arm on his shoulder and says, "Listen, kiddo. You have a second chance – don't screw it up. And if you need anything, I'm only one call away. Okay, come here."

He gives Richard hug and they're both overwhelmed with emotions. They pull away and Richard looks at Drake and says, "Thank you so much for everything you have done." Drake nods his head and Richard heads inside.

Drake looks at Rick showing dominance and tells him "You have a chance here, to do right by him. Do what you didn't do for us – just turn up and show support or you will have me to deal with."

Rick looks at him with pride and says, "You have my word. I will be a better father to him. Your mother would be proud of you." Drake and Rick embrace each other and then Rick goes inside the house. Drake looks at the house, like he can see into the future, thinking this is the start of something new.

Chapter 13

Drake is driving; he is nervous, and stuck on what he wants to say to Andrew. He has planned what he would say so many times but now that it's becoming a reality, he is stuck for words. Drake wants to know why there was a picture of him and his mother together. But Drake knew that he would have to meet him sooner or later, but he was hoping on the later.

Drake pulls up to a mansion on the outskirts of the city, guarded by a gate, preventing anyone from coming in. Drake pulls down the window and stretches out to hit a button.

Suddenly, there is buzzing sound, like a bee is attacking. The CCTV camera faces the car, and then the gates open sharply. Drake drives along the long road leading to the mansion. He pulls up outside. The mansion is a white coloured modern house, with fifty percent of the house having glass around it. He is panicking and shaking, knowing the time has come. He takes a breath in and out, and takes ten seconds to calm down.

Drake gets out of the car and walks towards the doors. He knocks on the door using the knocker, and the sound the knocker produces creates an echo. Suddenly, the door opens and a woman with blonde hair, brown eyes and wearing a leather jacket with black jeans opens the door. Drake notices who the woman is and reacts calmly to seeing her, and says, "Hello, Rebecca."

Rebecca looks at Drake, gives him a hug, and says, "How have you been, Drake?" She has a Scottish accent.

Rebecca Walters is Andrew Loid's bodyguard of twenty years. She worked for MI6 back in the day and when she got out Andrew hired her to be his bodyguard, even though he doesn't need one. Drake always got on with Rebecca back in the day. When Andrew sometimes used to cross the line, Rebecca would be the one to put him straight. She always understood Drake's frustration with Andrew, but she didn't know how to fix their relationship.

Drake responds in kind. "It's been a long two days. Been very stressful and I am tired, I've missed you, Rebecca."

Rebecca blushes; the two of them had always had a good relationship. She looks at Drake and responds, "It's been a while. Come on in – he's been expecting you."

Drake enters the mansion; they walk through the halls and the house is full of technology. Andrew has his own home digital servant. The house looks brand new on the inside, because he bought the land and built the house from scratch.

Drake gets chills from being back here – he doesn't like being reminded of who he was and this place is a big reminder. Rebecca and Drake approach a double door. Rebecca opens them both at the same time, revealing a study with a massive desk, a couch in the middle, and a coffee table, with two big bookshelves along the left side of the room.

Drake walks through the doors and notices a man standing at the bookshelves, wearing a black suit with long brown hair. He turns around showing his face; he has blue eyes and a scar along his cheek.

The guy standing firmly addresses Drake, saying in a British accent, "So you kept your promise."

Drake looks at him with anger, and says, "Hello Andrew."

Andrew lifts his hand in the direction of the chair telling Drake to sit. He looks at Drake with pure pride even though Drake despises him.

Andrew says, "I'm glad you're here."

Drake sits down in the chair and says sarcastically "I didn't have much of a choice, but I have something I wanted to ask you."

Andrew looks at him, reminiscing of old times. "You know it wasn't long ago when I came into your school and donated technology. But really, I was there to see what you were like."

Drake just came out and said what he felt and thought. "That's when my whole life changed; when you first approached me, saying you want to help mentor me. I didn't know I was actually being mentored by Nighthawk."

Andrew looks at Drake, curious if it was in a positive way. "Look I know I was hard on you; I know you didn't like how I did things, but I was trying to help you."

Drake's temper rises. He responds "You put me through hell. All I ever wanted to do was impress you, to make you proud of me and I never got that – just more commands."

Andrew sighs and looks at Drake. "You wanted to be strong. I gave you the tools to do that and I was proud of you and I gave you more tasks because I knew you were capable of accomplishing more. I also knew if I had showed you proudness or praised you, you would have weakened. So, yes, I was hard on you, but I always cared."

Drake looks at him, with a more understanding of why he acted the way he did. But now he had to get answers.

Drake says, "Back at the safe, where the cash was, I also saw an envelope in the safe. In the envelope, there was picture of you and my mother together. I want to know why."

Andrew looks at Drake and took a breath in and out knowing there is no easy way to tell him.

Andrew says "About a year before you were born, me and your mother, we, uh, knew each other. We were together. For a while we really loved each other. We went on holidays, which is where the photo was taken. But I became more distant due to my personal trauma of being in a hostage situation. I was going through PTSD."

Drake looks at him, surprised at what he is hearing;

Andrew continues. "Me and your mother had broken up by that time she met your father, Rick."

Drake is overwhelmed with what he is saying and responds, "Well now that clears that up. But why didn't you tell me?"

Andrew looks ashamed of himself and says, "Because I didn't think it mattered and I thought it was going to affect your training."

Drake scans Andrew's facial expression; he notices something and says to him, "There is still something you're keeping from me."

Andrew looks at him, panicking, not knowing how he is going to react, but tells him the full truth.

Andrew hands him an envelope. He says, "This was

given to me two weeks after your mother died."

Drake opens the envelope and reads the letter.

Andrew continues "I did the test; I couldn't believe it when I heard and I'm sorry you had to know so late."

Drake is absolutely shocked with what he has just read. He says, "No. This can't be – this isn't true!"

Andrew looks at him and says, "It's true. I am your biological father."

The End!